Noah The Snake at Large

by Henrietta Krumpett, illustrated by Monika Suska

Dedicated to Abigail, Gregory, and D.

Published by **KAMA** Publishing

19A The Swale, Norwich, NRS 9HE
www.kamapublishing.co.uk

British Library Cataloging in Publishing Data.
A catalogue record for this book is available from the British Library.

ISBN 978-0-9567196-7-6

Noah the Boa is found at the zoo.

He lives in the snake house on Floor Number Two.

He's looking at you.

Down in the snake house
it's time for a snack.

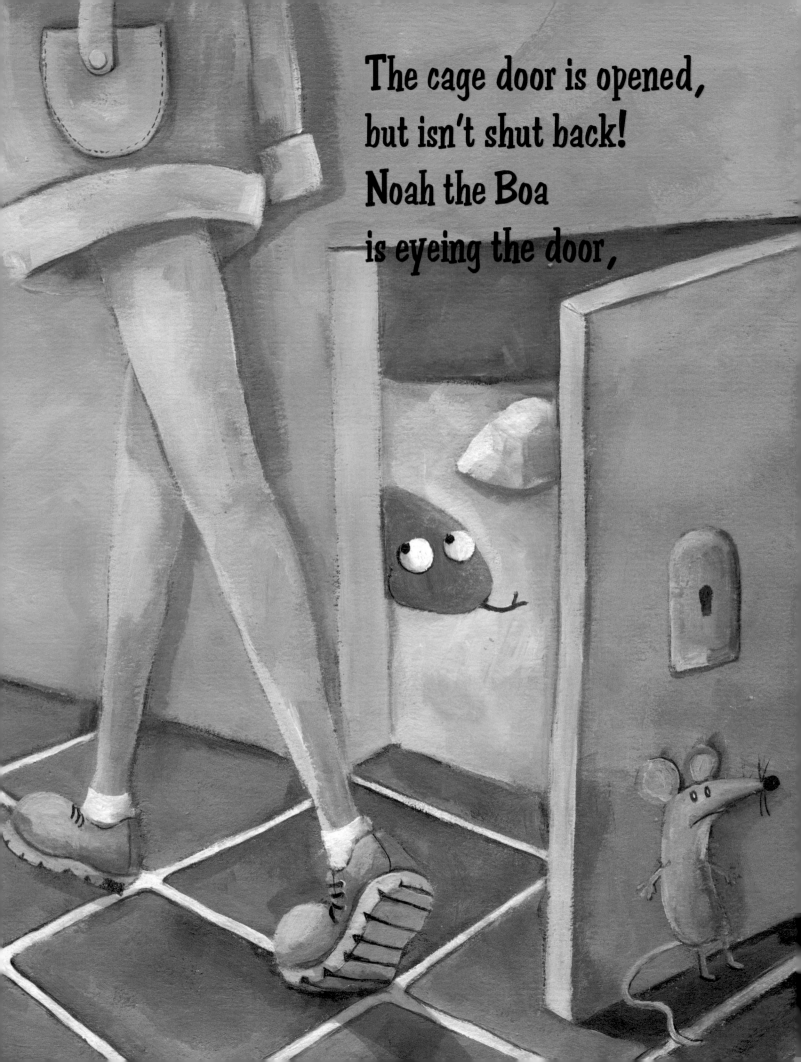

The cage door is opened,
but isn't shut back!
Noah the Boa
is eyeing the door,

watching and waiting
to slide on the floor,

at just the right time,
not a moment before.

Noah the Boa is slipping away,

sliding along with a swish and a sway,

slithering to the exit...

Hey!

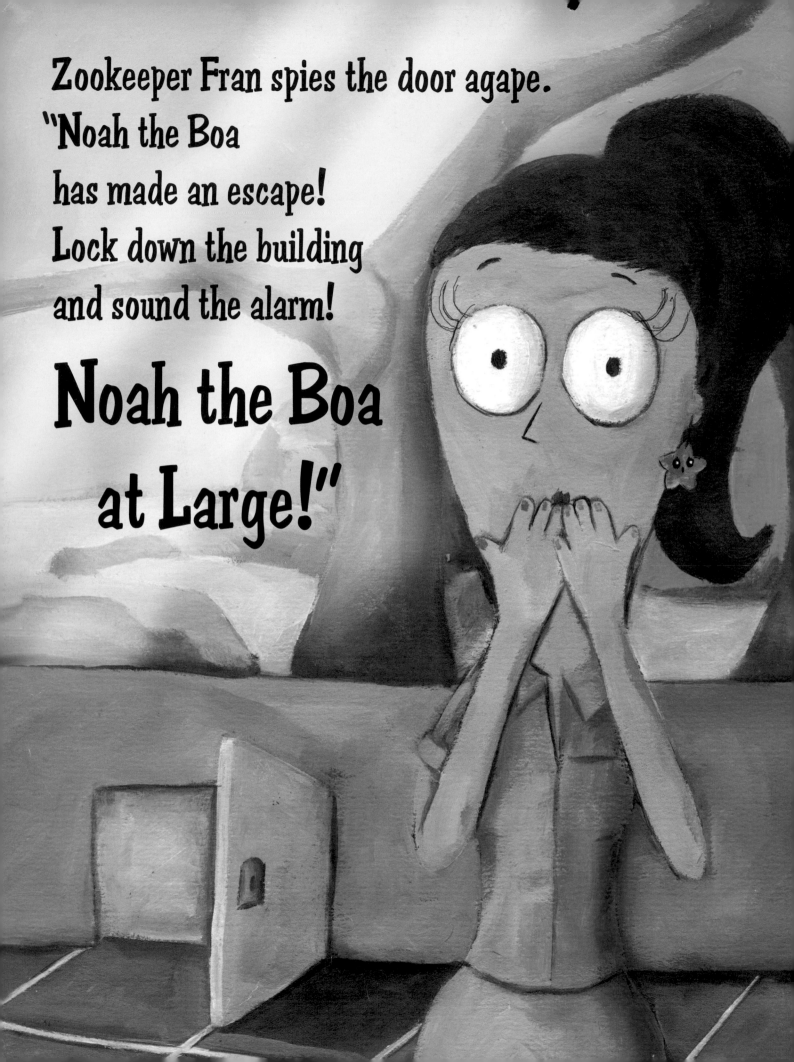

Zookeeper Fran spies the door agape.
"Noah the Boa
has made an escape!
Lock down the building
and sound the alarm!

Noah the Boa
at Large!"

Noah the Boa
is out on the street.
Watch out for the cars...

Wait, here's a taxi,
the windows are down.
The driver can't see him
and drives into town.

"That's my name," Noah smiles
and slips out of sight.

rolling into the coffee shop. People look. People stop.

Noah the Boa is getting away - into the movies - what's playing today?

He slithers onto an empty chair.
No one can see him. It's dark in there.

The movie is over and up people stand.
Who's beside Noah?
It's Zookeeper Fran!

"NOAH!" Zookeeper says with delight,
"I've been searching all over,
all day and all night!"

"I'm taking you back to the zoo on the double.
I can't have big snakes on the loose causing trouble!"
Zookeeper Fran leaves the movies in haste,
and Noah the Boa is wrapped round her waist.
"Noah, I have a surprise for you,"
says Zookeeper Fran when they get to the zoo.

"You have a new friend —
oh, yes, you do —
a beautiful red-tailed boa
named Lu!"
Noah the Boa
is happy to see
a brand new friend
curled up in his tree.

Noah the Boa
is found at the zoo.
He lives in the snake house
on Floor Number Two.

He's looking at Lu.